HORROR INSTINCT

TALES AND POEMS FROM THE GHOST WORLD

PRATEEK BANSAL

Copyright © Prateek Bansal
All Rights Reserved.

ISBN 979-888606450-6

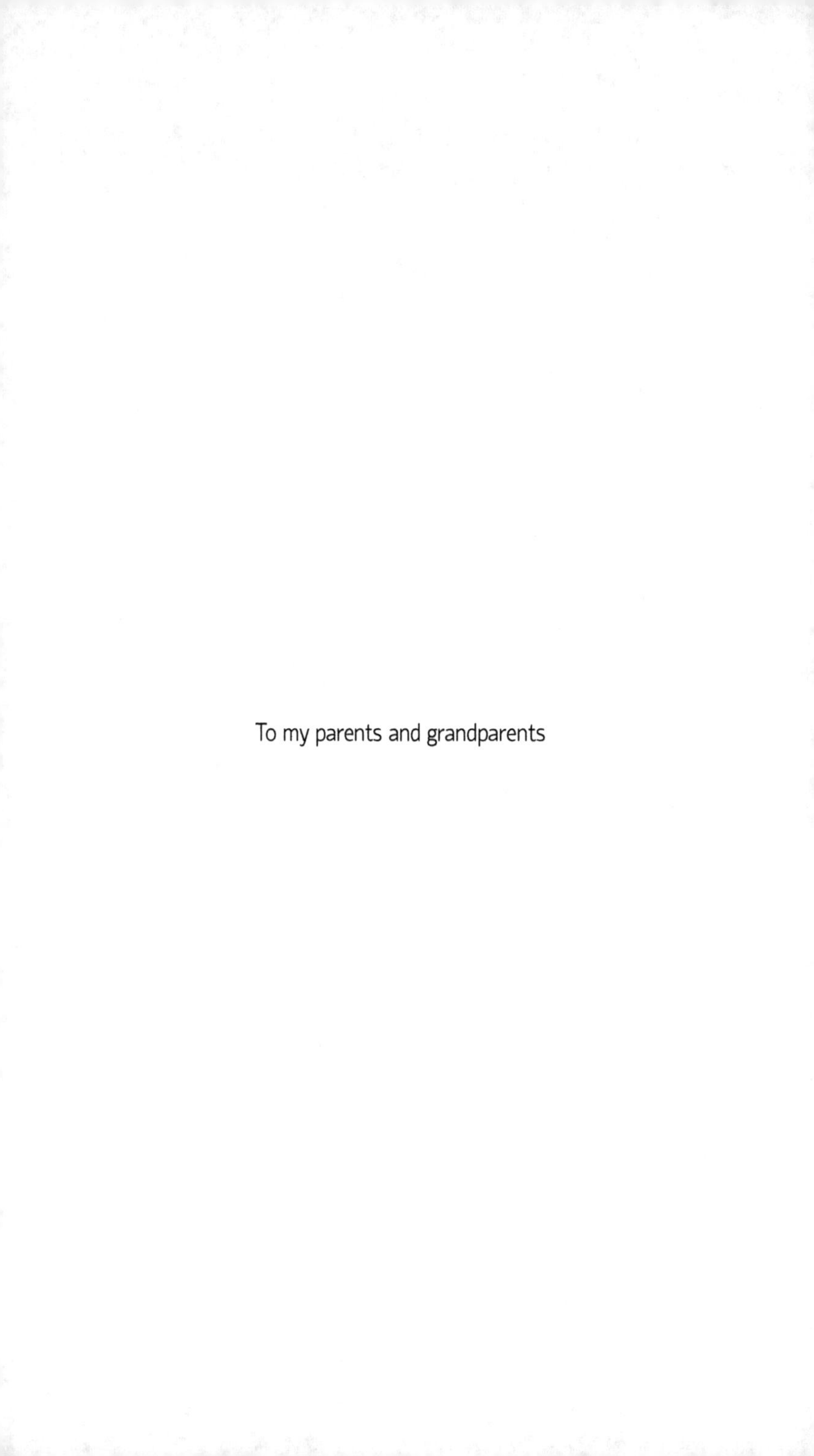

To my parents and grandparents

Contents

Preface

We have often heard of the supernatural powers and beings. Some say they dwell around us and some say they do not exist only. We are unaware of the truth. I personally believe in them. These stories and poems are based on the state of Himachal Pradesh. People say and I personally agree to it that ghosts and off course the Indian famous chudails are found there. The stories will take you to an exciting ride of thrillers of horror and will introduce you to all types of ghosts and faceless creatures and indian ghosts. I hope you enjoy it.

Acknowledgements

Firstly, I would like to thank my parents for the courage and support they have given me to complete these stories and poems. Then, I would like to thank the wonderful almighty for giving me the courage to complete this book. And I would also like to thank my grandparents for fully in favour of my passion. And who can forget the teachers, I would like to thank all my teachers. And then off course my dear friend, Harshal who always encourages me and motivates me and calls me 'Writer Sahab'. And I would like to thank all those who supported me and motivated me.

CHAPTER ONE

STORIES The Death of Night at Shimla

The hills of shimla are embedded with one of the most frantic terrors and possess the incidents which have given a way to the rise of supernatural belief and characters in the mind of the populace of the world. Only a few species can keep their body and souls together in this horror jungle where life is surrounded by solitary supernatural creatures which by contrast are not critters. But God has constructed some unique solitary creatures which give away their consternation to air and pull up courage from hell to behold themselves in front of these non alive creatures like mad.

One of my friends named Rahul Arora, a man of few words whose haphazard business had often brought him to the verge of ruin. He had turned up in goa with me and we had choreographed a visit to shimla which had gained momentum by a few of our other friends. Rahul Arora had concocted one of my best loved dishes which made their way from the south of India. I and Rahul sat on the table which was detected in the domicile of Rahul devouring the momentum gained dish. "What do you conjecture is Shimla an ideal place?" I said. "Positively" replied Rahul. "Ok then positively will go to Shimla." Before we made an appearance at Shimla I conjectured that all of us should convene at a restaurant and all of them did sympathize it. So we all took a chair at the table detected in the sea side restaurant of Goa possessed by Mr. Peck Hauchestoon drinking filtered coffee. Mr. Peck encountered us and we enlightened him with the particulars of the trip we had choreographed. "Shimla is a location with non alive homo sapiens" said he. "Just don't prate baloney" said one of our friends baptized Vivek Siddhi and Rahul sympathized it.And then finally we packed our valises and met at our hotel in Shimla where we would be facilitated with bed and breakfast It was at our atmos pleasure to be togetherRahul,Vivek,Arvind and me.

The hotel was assembled with old wood which manufactured a creaking sound at every pace.The hotel was manufactured on a titchy hummock among prodigious bens. The prodigious bens would seem like prodigious sorceress at the dead of night when chillness rules over the weather of Shimla and winds make paces at their fastest extent. The hotel was in the fashion of old british hotels of the seventeenth century. The hotel was itself a longevous one. We all were in a room of bewilderment in virtue of we were not certain that we were in the true hotel reserved by us.I till now was rebuking Vivek for his rudeness towards the direction of Mr. Peck Hauchestoon. We saw our accommodations which possessed british traits. The hotel possessed a restaurant,a bar and fifty sumptuous accommodations. On beholding the hotel it was like the fearful death of nights of Shimla which were possessed by stories and films had come to their lives and had commenced to make us frantic. That night when Arvind was taking a bath at his accommodation the water from the shower out of the blue stopped comming out. He looked at the shower and before he could say a knife red blood made it's way through the shower!! He bawled and came out of the accommodation in which dwelt and slipped on the floor. His head hit the floor at its greatest extentand bursted pouring blood over the floor of our dwelling place in Shimla. The episode was a very violent one and which could penetrate condolences from anyone's breast for Arvind who had turned up with us at Shimla.It was non-viable for any dwelling creature to engender such a horrendous act. It could only be a act of a non dwelling critter. We all were biding on the time when Arvind will roll up and then after holding our patience for a long time we started taking paces towards his room. And on beholding the horrendous field we all got frantic and astounded. It had seized our breath away.

The most pessimistic effect was that we were impotent to the situation.And then to awestruck us there was one more course of action attempted. A white coloured shroud arose and structured itself into a frock from which hands,legs and a horrendous face made it's way. The face had red eyes, hands and legs with prodigious nails. Blood was facilitating out from nose,eyes and ears.It was a lady face. She was looking like the lady which had brought the farm by falling from the hill of Shimla. She was a very non-ugly women from England. These particulars I conceived from thenewspaper the other day. I was gobsmacked on beholding such a terrific vision. Then out of the blue the lights started flickering. Then she started conquering on Arvind who had already kicked the bucket liquidating his non- soul body. After liquidating Arvind, she summoned the hotel workers by saying in a horrendous tone of voice "come everyone" and then again vociferated "come everyone!!" And everyone came-the manager, the waiter and everyone else who possessed faces without nose,eyes and ears!!Just blank monotonous and deadpan faces. I and Rahul commenced to run but Vivek was not able to run. It seemed that his legs had deceived him at the right jiffy. And then the ghost constructed her paces towards his direction.

"It is not baloney that ghosts draw breathe in this world"said the ghost to Vivek. Me and Rahul had to run, we didnot possessed any preferences. And then she came and catapulted Vivek towards the other faceless throng. They came and displayed their prodigious teeth and started masticating and triturating him. By the time any individual could say a knife he was devoured and only his bones could be viewed. And as we were running we recognized that there was no living creature in the hotel.....All of them were ghosts!!As we were taking fast paces the hotel transformed into a old rotten house possessing broken furniture,doors etc. The whole sight transformed into a black space. And then materialized the ghost in a black shadow that we could behold in front of us. With a prodigious knife of non blunt edge she manufactured paces towards our direction. We ran left but we could again behold her before us. She was vociferating at her highest extent of tone of voice"Dont run you wazzocks!! I will liquidate you!!" But nevertheless we kept our paces very fast towards the direction of right. And then a room on our left direction opened and Rahul went inside as if someone was pushing and pulling him inside. He was yanked inside. "Nooo!!" I vociferated but it was futile. And then after a minute or so the door opened. And it was far fetched what I saw, a skeleton came outside and commenced blabbering "I am Rahul Arora's skeleton, I have devoured him."

I ran like hell to the door which led to the out of the hotel and saw the skeleton in wake of me. And then kept on increasing the velocity of my paces. I was the only survivor left in virtue of others had been devoured by death. I kept on running and the finally appeared out of the hotel. My joy had no knowledge of its bounds. And then at the mid of the night I had to discover a source to reach the nearest destination. And then finally I found a horseless carriage passing by. I halted it and discovered a lady plonked inside. I asked her"Can you facilitate me with a lift??" and she replied"positively". And as I plonked inside I behold the women transforming into the ghost lady. Her eyes going red and the growth of prodigious nails. "You are dead you mad" she said to me and catapulted on me!

CHAPTER TWO

A Visit to the Mall Road

It is a fact that people proclaim that Shimla is embedded with supernatural characters and powers which make an individual frantic. And this is a story possessing the same traits. This story was told to me by my mater which now I am going to narrate to you. I oft have possessed the alacrity to ask the question whether this story is a fact one but no one has any answer to facilitate me. For my I possess that the story is a fact. This is how it begins:- Mrs. Prakash is sipping on hot coffee and talking to her friend. "What do you conjecture, shall we appear at the mall road tomorrow?" said Mrs. Kishore to Mrs. Bhushan. "Do you really want to appear ?" replied Mrs. Bhushan. "Positively....in virtue of it has been a long time" said Mrs. Kishore. "Ok we will positively appear" and saying this Mrs. Bhushan put down the call. Mrs. Bhushan had here house detected in one of the hummocks of the hills of Shimla. Mrs. Kishore also dwelt nearby only. That night when Mr. Bhushan arrived Mrs. Bhushan facilitated him with the particulars of the conversation. "Oh great" said Mr. Bhushan. The next day Mrs. Bhushan and Mrs. Kishore were dressed to visit the mall road. "Oh wow such beautiful objects are possessed by the mall road!!" exclaimed Mrs. Bhushan. There were jewellery shops, cloth shops, some spicy sapid north indian food selling vendors. Mrs. Bhushan and Mrs. Kishore possessed a mood which was very sapid. They commenced to spend money by shopping. By the contrast, this was conjectured by Mr. Bhushan and Mr. Kishore as waste of time and money. "Wow such exquisite ornaments!!" said Mrs. Kishore. "Positively" replied Mrs. Bhushan. By the time they had concluded their shopping it was evening and nightness and darkness had commenced to conquer the sky. It was getting dark and dwelling outside the domicile in the hills when darkness conquers makes an individual in peril. As both of them were paving their way to the parking lot of the mall road, a sound was facilitated to both of their ears. "Hault both of you !!" said the voice. They looked behind their backs and were gobsmacked on beholding that there was no one who possessed a place behind their backs . "Are we in a position were we possess peril?" said Mrs. Bhushan. " Negatively " replied Mrs. Kishore. " Ghosts donot dwell" perpetuated Mrs. kishore. And then when they turned front they beholded a sorceress. She possessed a prodigious white shroud with prodigious nails, red eyes and no nose and ears. She commenced to manufacture paces towards them. They were getting more and more frantic as she neared to them. It was the first of times of the lives of Mrs. Bhushan and Mrs. Kishore. When my mother set foot on this part of the story, even I also got frantic. Nevertheless Mrs. kishore and Mrs. Bhushan commenced to run at a sky scrapping velocity. Mrs. Bhushan was able to run but Mrs. Kishore's feet came across to be frozen!! She was not able to run at her velocity. Nevertheless Mrs. Bhushan ran and facilitated herself with a seat in their horseless carriage.

The sorceress facilitated her feet by paces which came across to be manufactured towards the direction of Mrs. kishore. Mrs. Kishore commenced to become frantic sanctioned and acknowledged that ghosts dwell. "It is not baloney that ghosts dwell" said the sorceress with a strong velocity of voice which by contrast was a blend of a men and women voice. She made her appearance in front of Mrs. Kishore and injected her prodigious nails into the stomach of Mrs. Kishore. Chiefly as Mrs. Kishore was facilitated by the prodigious nails, blood made it's way through her mouth. Her eyes commenced to bubble out as if they were going to blast. Her eyes also after a few jiffies led out blood out of her. While this field was transpiring, Mrs. Bhushan ran in a frenzy with her horseless carriage. Mrs. Kishore had commenced bringing the farm. And then concludally, she brought the farm. The sorceress had liquidated Mrs. Kishore. The incident could penetrate condolences from anyone's breast. Mrs . Bhushan perpetuated to run in her horseless carriage. She ran through the small passage of the parking lot and onto the road which led to her domicile. Mrs. Bhushan perpetuated to run unless she was haulted by a figure in front of her which looked like a figure after the fashion of shadows. It was like a prodigious shadow. She had herself struck by franticness. Then she beholded that the figure out of the blue dissapeared. Then when she beholded her mirror she saw that the figure was seated on the back seat of her horseless carriage. She vociferated and ran out of the horseless carriage. Her run possessed the sky scrapping velocity of her. And then she felt that she was being lifted by someone but there was no one lifting her!! She was flying in the air on her own!! And then she saw that blood was comming out of her nose,eyes and ears making her frantic. And out of the blue she felt that she was being stretched and then she blasted with blood all over. Her body parts - lungs, heart , hand and legs had fallen in different locations!! Only blood could be beholded. And Mr. Bhushan was comming from his office to his domicile and on beholding such a horrendous field he was facilitated with a heart attack! And to this day some people hold in their minds that this was a real incident. And on hearing this line till date I possess the fear of roaming in the hills and hummocks of Shimla after six in the evening.

CHAPTER THREE

A Robber's Experience

Raghav, a robber had decided to break in today at the big white house located in Manali. The house belonged to one of the oldest families who lived there. Raghav had the bad habit of stealing from other's houses. He had robbed a number of houses in Shimla, chail and many other towns and cities of Himachal Pradesh. He was often caught but escaped. Now, he wanted to steal from the very famous white house of Manali. He quietly walked around the house and reached at the backside of the large abode. It was night twelve and the winds were fast and cold. The chilness of the hills could be discerned. He silently climbed up the back wall of the house. With great difficulty in climbing the long and mammoth wall, he entered the premises of the house. Raghav saw a view of beautiful flowers and trees that grew in the back garden. Raghav switched on the torch he had brought and picked up a bunch of white lily flowers for his wife, Shanti. He had told his wife a lie that he used to work in a hotel and she was unaware of the truth that he was a burglar. He walked and reached to a window of the mammoth house. He broke open the window and jumped inside. He landed into a bedroom which was empty. It was probably a guest room, he thought. He walked out of the room and saw a very palatial and luxurious living room in the light of his torch. The beautiful and royal furniture with designer and expensive vases and furniture. The sound of the pendulum clock scared Raghav as it struck to twelve fifteen. Suddenly, a shadow passed behind him. He got scared and turned behind to see who it was. But it was no one. He opened a bag which he had bought with him and commenced to put all the royal and expensive furniture in the bag. The vases where made of real gold and decorated with expensive stone jewels. And then suddenly, a old woman comes and says, "What are you doing?" She switch on all the lights and chandeliers. "I...I..," Raghav did not do what to say. "Don't you dare take my furniture," saying this she came with a stick to hit Raghav. "No!" Said Raghav as he defended himself from the attack. He pushed aside the old woman and she fell aside. He took the bag and fled with all the possible furniture he could keep his hand on. The old woman kept shouting, "Don't you dare take my furniture." Raghav ran and came out of the premises of the mammoth and luxurious house through great difficulty by jumping out of the window and climbing up the wall. As he walked outside, he just wanted to see what he had caught his hand on. He opened the bag and was shocked. There were only rocks in it and no furniture. The rocks were worth nothing! "What is this?!" Raghav exclaimed. Raghav found a paper in the bag and he opened it and found written in it "Don't you dare take my furniture". Raghav was shocked. And then he realized that someone had plunged a sword in his stomach! He turns behind and finds the old woman saying, "Don't you dare take my furniture!" Raghav was dead now. The police found his body with knife marks and blood all over. Shanti could not think why anyone would kill her husband. And it was not 'anyone' it was a supernatural being, probably a ghost.

CHAPTER FOUR

Sisters and Daughters

Mrs. Maduri is lying on her death bed. She has cancer and is taking her last breath. She has her both daughters by her side, Tanya and Tara. Tanya is elder, of twenty - five while Tara is smaller, of twenty. Mrs. Maduri was a rich lady, earned more money that enjoyed her life. Her life was now comming to a conclusion for the same reason as her husband - the cancer. She had lot of properties in Shimla as well as in the whole state of Himachal Pradesh. She was speaking her last words. "Take care!" After saying this she was in difficulty to breathe and gasped, filled her lungs as much as she could but she had to go. She left. Her children crying, making sorrow of a great loss. They were only in their young ages and their mother was gone. Gone forever. Both of the daughters, Tanya and Tara could not stop weeping. Now, the will of the mother says that the property and wealth splits into half. They were very well - healed. If the property was divided into two also, both of them would have enough and a lot. They did the last rites and people started visiting. People started to act smart saying like, "You should start earning and not spend the money that your mother has left," "Tanya should have the whole share of the wealth and properties, Tara is 'very' small now," and what not. But never was in the knowledge of anyone that Tara has a dark side. She hated her elder sister. She thought that Mrs. Maduri and her long gone father loved Tanya more than her. But it was never so. Tara decided something vicious, something never could anyone imagine that she could do. To murder her own elder blood, Tanya. She had the greed to get all the property and thought that this is the best time to take the revenge of all the things she thought to be unfair. The day had ended, all the people were gone and would return the next day. One of Tara's aunts had also offered to stay there but how could she carry out her plan with a second person in the house? She also had many servants but they would go to their quarters at the back of the house by night. Then she would be alone and will also have enough time to kill her sister, Tanya. Now it was only Tara and Tanya and an intention to kill. Tara was deciding how could she kill her elder sister before the sun would rise. She had to do something. Firstly, she decided that she would lock the door which led to the servant's quarter. And then she decided that she would kill her sister by putting a cushion over her head and then hang her by the fan to show that she had suicided. But wouldn't it be obvious that she had murdered. She had a solution for it, she would write a letter that Tanya had killed herself because she had found from a old diary of their mother that she was adopted and Tanya could not handle the truth so she killed herself. It was the perfect reason she thought. She did as decided, locking and killing and hanging. She was happy after doing this and felt content. The next morning when Tara got up she was gobsmacked. She saw Tanya making breakfast. How was she alive? What had happened when she killed Tanya? How was she alive? "Oh My God!" Whispered Tara to herself. She could not believe her eye balls. What was happening? She wondered. She ran to the bathroom in her luxurious room and washed her face a dozen times. She was gobsmacked! And then she saw in the mirror her mother! She turned back and her mother was standing right there! She shouted. "No one can hear you," said the ghost of her mother. "You always thought we loved your sister more than you. It was never true. And this is the fact that you are adopted. We had found you when we were traveling by road. You were in your real mother's hand when the bus you were traveling in met with an accident. We adopted you from then," continued the ghost of the mother. Tara was shocked. The ghost of Mrs. Maduri continued, "There was no need to do what you had done. Tanya also knows that you are adopted but she did not love you any less. I made Tanya alive. That is my supernatural power. I just wanna say don't mess anything." And the ghost vanished into thin air. Tanya did not remember anything what had happened with her. That was the power of supernatural. She went to call her sister, Tara for breakfast. She was not there in her room. She knocked the door of her bathroom. There was no response even after a hundred knocks. She called one of the servant and broke open the door. Tara had killed herself. Tara could not believe what she had seen and herd from the ghost. She could not stomach it. She killed herself. Now, the whole wealth belonged to Tanya.

CHAPTER FIVE

Highway Narration

Rishabh was driving the car on the highway to Kochi from Bengaluru. He was with his wife, Ankita. They used to and liked to travel in night. Rishabh would sleep before they left for Kochi and so he could drive the car at night. This was Ankita's idea. The road was dark and silent. If anybody would drop a pin, the sound of the action could be discerned, that's how silent the highway was. They were moving frantically. They did not know what they were going to do now. They were just frightened. Why? No one knew except themselves. They had stains of blood on their car wheel. Small yet significant and visible stains of blood. As if they have ran over some animal in the dark. Or a human being? Ankita asked, "What to do now?" "How do I say?" Replied Rishabh. "You only speeded up the car!" She vociferated. "No! You told me to do so," defended Rishabh. "Oh God!" Exclaimed Ankita. It was a few crummy hours before when they had just started traveling. The journey from Bengaluru to Kochi is of eight to ten hours by car. It was just two hours at twelve in the night when they had entered the highway. The highway was quite long. They did not know what to do and what not to do. They could be accused of a murder and what not, they commenced to imagine every possible consequences and difficulties they will have to or may have to face. Rishabh was searching beside the car, behind the car to look for any animal, creature or human he would discover injured or.....dead. "I am walking a little further," said Rishabh to Ankita. "Why?" Asked Ankita. "Are you dumb?" "What?!" "I am going to see if the body of a human.....or whatever is fallen somewhere further." "You think it's an human?" "Do you think I am an astrologer? How will I know without seeing?" "OK! but come fast!" Rishabh was walking slowly and attentively, looking in all possible directions. Walking and walking in the silence of the darkness. And then, what he sees? A body of man lying in front of him covered with blood. The red face and body of the lying man were frantic making. Rishabh was terrified. He went near the body and shaked it to see if the he was alive. "Sir!sir!" He spoke while shaking. He was getting more terrified. The person was dead! He was damn scared. He ran towards the car as fast as he could. "Ankita! Ankita!" He came running. Ankita could see him from far. She was trying to understand what had happened. She came out of the car and run towards Rishabh. "What happened?" She asked. "The man.... man is dead," he replied. "What?!" "Yes!" "Now, what should we do?" "I don't know, but we are for sure in a mess." "Oh my God!" "Wait! What is that behind you?" Asked Rishabh when he saw a black shadowy figure comming behind Ankita. He saw it clearly as it approached them. It was the dead man covered with blood throughly. "Oh! No!" Exclaimed Rishabh. "What?" Asked Ankita. "It is this man who was dead! How is he alive? And why is he comming towards us?!" "What?!" "Run!" They ran. And ran. And ran. He was comming towards them. And his hand possessed a knife. Where did he get it from? Was he a fisherman? They did not know anything. Just run for you lives! He was running behind them. And then they see, he is not behind them. Where is he then? They saw and were shocked, they had reached back near their car, from where they had started running. And again saw the man comming and running behind them with his sword. What was happening? The next day in the newspaper, it was printed that a couple driving a car through the highway are missing. Only the car is found but not the couple. What is the truth? We don't know. And we also don't know who killed whom?

CHAPTER SIX

A Hospital to Remember for

" I saw her, with my own pair of circles!" Said the patient terrified. "What did you saw?" Asked Vandana, the nurse. "A terrifying women with mushroomed hair, long nails, red eyes and blue tongues saying that she will take my new born." "Oh! Really?" Asked Vandana as if mocking. "Ya..please do something sister!" "It must for sure be a bad dream and it will also be bad if you conjecture about it, just sleep now. Being awake for a long time will affect you," saying this Vandana left the ward of the hospital on the hills of Shimla. She was wondering why Mrs. Joseph was saying so, was that real? Mayhap a dream, she though not to conjecture of it again and get back to work and finish what had been alloted for the night shift. Checking the ICU ward, the blood pressure and sugar and oxygen level of certain patients, everything was done by three in the morning. Vandana was tired and went into the staff room where she meet Hema. "How was your night?" Asked Hema. "Not great. Just the same old work and fashion," came the reply. "Nothing extraordinary?" "There was this one patient, speaking about the ghosts and such halloween stuff." "Mrs. Joseph?" "Ah..yes! Mrs. Joseph!" "She is always like that since three days." "Any particular reason?" "No, I don't know." "God knows! But I have heard that this hospital was or is haunted, is that true?" "Oh no. They just tell that because a peepal tree was cut to make this hospital. They consider that to be a bad omen, you must be knowing, right?" "Hmm...yaa," replied Vandana as if in a deep - deep thought. "And you know where the peepal tree was situated?" "Where?" Asked Vandana immediately, showing interest. "Right where we keep new born babies." "Oh my God! So scary! But by the way how do you know all this Hema?" "I am have been working in this for three solid years, what do you expect?" "OK." Vandana was a new nurse in the hospital, she did not have the knowledge about all such 'halloween' stuff. She was told that the hospital was haunted but in virtue of her financial condition, she had to take the step. Vandana was wondering all the stories and was tired so she dozed off. There was a sudden bang on the door of the staff room which made Vandana open her eyes wide enough. She got up frightened. What was it? Why was it? She went upto the door of the room and opened it. She was terrified. She could not believe what she had seen. A hollow ghostly figure was standing it front of her. Scattered hair, red eyes and every freaking trait of a ghost. It was Mrs. Joseph. "I told you," she said in a frantic making voice. "I had told you." Vandana screamed. "No one can hear you here," came the ghostly reply. She continued screaming. Mrs. Joseph came running to her and as Vandana moved, Mrs. Joseph crashed into the computer monitoring the patients. "Aaaaaaa......" she shouted and ran towards Vandana again. Vandana could not believe it. Vandana was flabbergasted. Mrs. Joseph jumped and sprouted on the frightened nurse. She ate her, in the most ruthless way. Blood was everywhere, on the walls of the room, like everywhere. Vandana got up from her dream, it was a frightening dream and nothing else. She was relieved and calm. What she had seen was the worst dream she would have had. What a night! Vandana came out of the staff room and saw that there was a crowd gathered outside the mother's ward, where the mothers after delivering were admitted. She went there and saw that Mrs. Joseph was dead. She was in the same condition as Vandana had seen in her dream. Red eyes, weird hair. Vandana's jaw fell down. What she had seen was a dream or reality? What was the mystery? Thousands of questions erupting in her mind with no answer. Vandana would never ever forget this hospital in her life. It would be a hospital to remember for.

The Horrendous Domicile

It was a solitary incident which made its appearance at our bunglow in Bengaluru. The man who was holding our objects which were declared to be shifted at our new domicile in Shimla fell and along with him our objects also made their way to the ground."Be guarded" I said in a prudent fashion. My sister baptized Shweta and I used to dwell in our Dmicile of Bengaluru. But since I had been facilitated by a order of transfer by my company, my sister and me were positive on the choreograph to shift to Shimla.And then finally my sister and me were ready to depart for Shimla. We had transported all the objects possessed by us to Shimla. And after two days we had departed to Shimla and had commenced settling at Shimla. And before we had made an appearance at Shimla, we had conceived a lot of stories possessing ghosts which had made my sister frantic. "No complications are available to worry about" I said soothing her. And then as we stepped foot on our pristine domicile and opened the door it manufactured a creaking sound which was cromulent to make my sister frantic. "I hope it is negative that the ghosts dwell here" she said to me. "Off course negative" I replied. And then our belongings were positioned at their seasonable places. And then as we entered a cold breathe rushed over us. We opened the windows to save the domicile's backbone from damp. It was our first night at the new domicile. As I was seated on a couch reading a book when out of the blue two hands made their appearance and commenced sucking me into the couch. I became frantic and then shouted to recognize it was a dream. I got up from my pleasure loving sleep with a shout. My sister sleeping adjacent to me got up and called out" all ok right?" and I replied "positive.....was facilitated with a horrendous dream." The next morning we had facilitated ourselves with breakfast not from home but from external of the domicile. It was fresh omelets concocted by a known chef of Shimla. We also devoured breads along with omelets. "What succulent and appetizing omelets!" I exclaimed. My sister also got a soft spot for omelets. After that I went for my work on account of which we had shifted to Shimla. My sister beholded the storeroom which was detected at the backside of the house. There was a small door like opening which led to a old road of Shimla and a small woods on our dwelling hummock. My sister passed through the opening and came out beholding the vintage street and a path which led to the woods in the hummock. My sister commenced manufacturing paces towards the woods and as she was walking a little man dressed with a brown rotten coat, a white but begrimed shirt and a pair of pale blue briefs appeared a commenced to shout"you and your brother will bring the farm soon." My sister on getting frantic posted a slap on the wazzock's face and vociferated"Get lost you idiot." And then before any individual could utter a knife the man dissapeared. She was awe stricken on beholding the sudden disappearance nevertheless she commenced to run back towards our domicile but was gobsmacked on beholding the domicile was not there in its detected place!! My sister had became very frantic and had commenced to run towards the old vintage road hoping to find some solution. She was assuming herself in peril in virtue of she thought that a ghost was behind her and she had to save her back. And then the old vintage road welcomed her into herself. It was after the fashion of roads of the eighteenth century. It had prodigious trees on its edge. My sister beholded a tree and became frantic in virtue of she saw a women hanging from it with her eyes crushed and tongue out of the mouth. And then to her ears came a sound which vociferated"stop Shweta, it will make you in peril if you are negative in being stationary." And the she saw behind, she beholded the same lady hanging on the tree!! She saw the tree, and there was negative a women hanging from its branches. The sorceress was dressed in black gown with red eyes and prodigious nails. She was manufacturing paces towards my sister making her frantic.My sister was not able to manufacture paces, her legs seemed frozen!! She was comming oh really she was comming making my sister frantic. She came nigh to my sister and crushed my skin and blister's eyes. And then shoved my skin and blister and wedged her nails into my skin and blister's body. Skin and blister of mine had brought the farm!! The girl who had facilitated my sister with ever sleeping illness dwelt in our domicile during the 90's. That night when I made my appearance at my horrendous domicile, I discovered that my sister had evanesced. I also went through the passage and then to the vintage road possessing some alacrity to discover something paving the way towards my skin and blister. And I found nothing but her dead body. I was crying to extent of my sorrow. It was like my backbone had brought the farm. I had cremated her by the next day and had decided to leave Shimla. My flight back to Bengaluru was that evening itself. I had wrapped up all the objects possessed by me and was dressed to make an appearance at Bengaluru. I took the taxi and reached the airport by four in the evening. Finally I was ready to depart for Bengaluru. I was leaving Shimla with sorrowful mind and had decided to take up a new function after appearing at Bengaluru. I sat on board and the characteristics of flight safety were set on commencing. The flight was on air after a few jiffies. And then a voice called me back and I saw back and was gobsmacked on beholding that the individual who called me possessed no facial characteristics- no eyebrows, no ears , no eyes!! And then I looked all around myself and saw that all individuals around me possessed same faces. "You have to die, you wazzock" said a voice and I recognized that I was getting a heart attack!!

CHAPTER EIGHT

The Strange Neighbourhood

Mrs. Clare's car drove through the misty hills. She was moving with her son and daughter into her new abode. The new abode was in a small village on the Himalayan hummocks. The village comprised only a small bunch of abodes with only a populace of fifty or even less than that. Everyone conjectured that the village was on the verge of bankruptcy but it was not so. The people in the village possess the knowledge how to manage the scenario. They have certainly managed it pretty well. Now a plot was there in the village, pretty well off. Mrs. Clare was assigned by her company in the virtue of analyzing the land so that her fabric company could establish a factory at a cheap price. Mrs. Clare, a fair complexion woman with a small but elegant nose and a lanky and ravishing body, got down the car to sight her new abode. The two children also got down. The daughter was eight and the son eleven. They both were like their mother, ravishing and fair complexion. They stood as they witnessed their abode. It was a small three bedroom one, with a small kitchen and a medium extended hall. It had a small front lawn which was bewitching as there were flowers, grown and maintained by the possessor of the abode. Now, it was Mrs. Clare's responsibility. The man from the neighbouring abode came and said, " Are you Mrs. Clare?" "Yes", came the reply from her. "Oh! Welcome to our small yet elegant village. I am the possessor of the abode that you are about to move in and if you would excuse, I can get the keys." Mrs. Clare nodded, and the man, Johnson went into his abode to fetch the keys. Johnson was of fifty though he did not look like. He was a man of great personality and virtues. He materialized with the keys and guided the three to the path of the abode. Mrs. Clare had discerned that the small village was manifested by ghosts and that all the people who went there would with no doubt kick the bucket. Mrs. Clare weened that this was nothing but baloney. She was a woman who did not believe the dwelling of super natural beings. And without even thinking twice, she came to the place. Do ghosts dwell there? If yes then how to the people dwell there? People that disappeared here were taken by ghosts? Everything was a mystery. Mrs. Clare's only mistake was that she forgot to see that Johnson did not possess any shadow. It was eight in the night and the family of the three were seated on the dinning table. The kids had come without a scream, presumably because they had just came into their new abode and would come down. They had just put the mattresses and decided they would place the rest of the furniture the next dawn. Mrs. Clare had lot of work to do the next dawn. She had to get the children admitted to the only school on the hummock, get the furniture detected on the right location and to even acquaint with people in the small town on the hummocks of the Himalayan hills. The previous individuals who dwelt here, had left some of their furniture which also had to be cleared. The next day, Mrs. Clare made the children get up by six and took them to school. They would be facilitated with education in that school after the next week, when the new term would commence. Mrs. Clare had felt strange because when she asked to the neighbor adjacent, " How are you?" She did not get any response other than a monotonous look as if she was a dead spirit. Again Mrs. Clare's mistake, she forgot to see the shadow less neighbour. Mrs. Clare commenced to see the old furniture which the previous dwellers had left. She commenced with a table which possessed a mirror and drawers on either side of it. The mirror looked antique. In fact, the whole system of the table looked after the fashion of Britishers of the eighteenth century. "How come such an old piece of furniture comes to bide here?" Muttered Mrs. Clare to herself. She commenced to check the drawers. She even found an eighteenth century locket with a photo in it. The photo was of a lady, nigh to thirty. Mrs. Clare searched more and also found a diary. The cover of the diary was of brown leather. The diary also resembled the eighteenth century era. She was about to open it, when the lad and lass came running. They were fighting for a toy, so she kept the diary aside and decided to evaluate their fright before it alters itself into a mess. That night, after supper Mrs. Clare sitting on her mattress, opened the diary. It was like a journal from within. Mrs. Clare opened a middle page and commenced to read. It read as follows: 16th July, 1678 Today is a very solitary day, I don't know why. It seems to me that every personality in this village is dead. I don't know the acknowledgment for which I ween this. But, no one responds even to a blithe hi. What is transpiring in this village? I don't know. Mrs. Clare read it and hacked back a day before, when Johnson had told her that a lady who dwelt here was found dead on 17th July, 1678. Was it this lady only? And how did Johnson know that, presumably he wasn't born even then? All was a mystery. As Mrs. Clare put down the diary, she saw Johnson standing in front of her! But something was strange, he had bloody hands and legs! His eyes were blank and bleeding! His face was black! He said, " You came to know the truth." Saying so he jumped on her and with no doubt liquidated her into small pieces by biting. Of the fifty dead people or precisely souls, a collection of three were added. The whole village was dead. Now, it had fifty - three souls, waiting for more.

CHAPTER NINE

The Creepy Road

The road was horrendous. The road was terrific. The road was manifested by ghosts. The road had frightened the entire populace. The road was in Shimla. After the death of the day, at the jiffy when the entire metropolis of Shimla was asleep, the ghosts that manifested the road, so horrendous, would commence to wander about. Some faceless, some with red plasma manifested face and eyes, some with the horrendous complexion of the most frantic making fashion. Some as fair as a lychee, and some as red as an apple. Some with up side down fashioned feet and some with mammoth nails to tear any personality into two halves. The populace had even discovered blood shattered on the roads. They conjectured that presumably a man, who had come alone on the road, was teared side ways by a solitary fashioned feet of a chudail. It was an irregular mystery. A pool of red and frantic making blood, the disappearance of a woman, every single thing was a unique and solitarily a mystery. The local inspector with the weight of the area on his shoulders, could not evaluate the episodes even after perpetually investigating. Especially on the nights of amavasya, people were unconventionally frantic. The people dwelling near the road thought that the ghosts would come beyond the road and materialize into their abode. So as a consequence, they would embark all possible signs of their respective religion on their main doors and lock the doors as if they had sighted a yegg the previous day. Nandu, a twenty man in life, dwelled with his mother. Nandu was a lanky man with a fair complexion face and body. He possessed a handsome body and a tenebrous pair of orb. He and his mother shared a pre - eminent relationship. They loved each other at the highest level. Nandu was a man of great virtues, he served his mother. He functioned on every possible thing that would make his mother blithe. Every one in their neighborhood, wondered how Nandu had loved his mother and how much compassion and affection he possessed towards her direction. His father had kicked the bucket when he had just ran across ten. His mother had taken care of him in the most optimal fashion. From that very day, the mother son shared the most optimal love. Nandu had just come from his office, it was nine in the dark of night. He entered and sighted that his mother was concocting chicken. He could discern the sound of the vessels. He came into his room and commenced to refresh by taking off his tie. He was going to take off his shirt when he heard the shout of his mother. He ran towards the kitchen where his mother was concocting chicken. He saw that his mother was on the ground, holding her hand near her chest. He came to know that his mother was getting a heart attack. He held his mother on his back, put him in his old but good horseless carriage. He ran his horseless carriage at a speed of hundred. His mother could not bear. The scenario was getting out of his hand. He decided with certainty that he would take the creepy road which was a shortcut to the nearest hospital. He took the car to creepy and mysterious road, which was manifested by ghosts and divurgent chudails. He possessed no other choice. He drove at the maximum speed he could. The road was very dingy and murky. Nandu looked at the rear mirror and he could not believe what he had beholded. He saw a woman, with red eyes and mammoth nails and her feet up side down! Blood was pouring down from her eyes and through her fleshy cheeks. She was lanky, creepy and horrendous. Her vampire like teeth could freak anyone. Nandu ran the car, his mother moaning because of the pain. Nandu was looking back and missed to see front in the fog, he turned his head and sighted a ghost. A ghost that looked old, possessed eyes with no eye balls. His head commenced to rotate, round and round. He turned the car and dashed into a tree. The headlights were bursted and the road had become stygian. Nandu got out of his car, coughing. He ran to the other side of the car and his mother was lying with closed eyes. He weened that his mother had died. He commenced to bawl and cry. Then, he felt that his mother was shaking. He opened the door and touched his mother by shoulder and commenced shaking. In a fraction of a jiffy, his mother got up. She had no eyes. It was blank. Her mouth was bleeding! She took her hand and posted it on Nandu's neck and commenced to choke him. He shouted. He called for help. There was no one. His mother lifted her hand and her nails began to grow to a mammoth size. Her body was manifested by the horrendous chudail. She pricked the bunch of nails into Nandu's body. Blood commenced to come out of his body, mouth and eyes. Blood was shattered all over the street. The local inspector had discovered one more case to ponder upon. Two bodies were discovered, one of sixty and other twenty thrashed in the most bad and callous fashion.

CHAPTER TEN

POEMS A Roaming Ghost

A ghost, roaming,
  A ghost so frightening,
  A ghost embedded in the hills,
  To welcome the sweet and frantic chills.
  A ghost with no complexion,
  A ghost so stygian.
  A ghost, roaming,
  A ghost for preying,
  A hunt for a predator,
  Any of a kind predator.
  A ghost roaming,
  To capture a human being.

CHAPTER ELEVEN

Who is there?

A rumour of fame,
    A rumour of scare,
    A rumour of ghosts,
    A rumour of chills,
    Dwelt a ghost frightens,
    The rumour was.
    A man passing the area,
    Discerned the noise of ghostly era,
    He the rapid fashion out walked,
    The noise was going loud,
    Again he walked,
    Again the noise pitched.
    Could not bear it he,
    Got a Heart attack and died he,
    What to the unfortunate lads,
    And lasses know the consequences?
    Who were behind this act of scare,
    That the man could die.

CHAPTER TWELVE

Don't Kill Her

A man so callous,
   A man so heartless,
   Killed a lizard out of fun,
   What damned it was fun?
   Bravery on a small creature,
   He would repay in sure.
   That night, fast was he snoring,
   When a dream so frightening,
   His wits approached,
   So was he dumbfounded,
   That day, nor this day,
   He would kill not a lizard surely.

CHAPTER THIRTEEN

A Knock on the Door

A knock on the door,
   A knock at late an hour,
   A knock so solitary,
   A knock so scary,
   An individual inside.
   Took to open the door wide.
   The door ajar with glinting,
   A lamp of a human being,
   Stood a lady with sweet fashion,
   Was she really in breathing fashion?
   No she was nt, domsday was for,
   The people inside had welcomed a ghost, unt for prey
for.